A B C D 1 2 3 4

WALT DISNEY's
THE ARISTOCATS

GROLIER
BOOK CLUB EDITION

Published in the United States by Grolier Enterprises Inc., Danbury, Connecticut.
Originally published in Denmark by Egmont Books, Copenhagen, in 1994.

"Marie, you are going to be as beautiful as your mother," said Madame. "Isn't she, Duchess?"

Duchess smiled. She and her three kittens lived with Madame in a beautiful house in Paris. The cats loved Madame, and she loved them.

The kittens were very talented.
Toulouse was learning to paint.

Marie was learning to sing.

And Berlioz was
learning to play the piano.

Madame appreciated the kittens' talent. But Edgar the butler did not appreciate the mess they made.

"I am not a butler," he grumbled to himself. "I am a cat-sitter for four spoiled Aristocats."

One day Madame's lawyer stopped by for a visit.

"George, I would like to leave my fortune to my beloved cats," Madame told him. "I'm sure Edgar will be glad to take care of them when I am gone."

Edgar heard everything Madame said. But he was not glad at all!

"Those cats must go," Edgar muttered.

That night the greedy butler put sleeping pills in the cats' cream!

"A slip of the hand, and it's off to dreamland," he chuckled. The pills went *plip-plop!* into the pot.

"I'll take them far away. Then Madame will leave her fortune to me."

Dinner was delicious! The cats gladly shared it with their friend Roquefort the mouse.

Roquefort dipped his cracker into the bowl. "*Mmm*, my compliments to the chef," he said.

"It's crème à la Edgar," Marie told him.

Roquefort went to get another cracker. But he fell asleep as soon as he reached his hole.

Soon all the cats were sound asleep, too. Edgar carefully put them in their basket. Madame had gone to bed. The house was quiet.

Edgar drove the cats far away from the city.

"These cats will never find their way back to
Paris," the butler said to himself.

Edgar's noisy motorcycle rumbled along the road.
But Duchess and her kittens didn't wake up.

Suddenly the motorcycle hit a large bump in the road. Edgar's hat flew off his head! The basket full of sleeping cats bounced out of the sidecar. It landed under a bridge. But Edgar didn't stop. Instead he hurried back to the city.

When they woke up the next morning, Duchess and the kittens had a very unpleasant surprise.

"Where are we, Mama?" asked Toulouse.

"Don't worry, children," Duchess assured them. "I will find a way for us to get back to Madame."

But she did not know what to do.

Just then Duchess saw another cat. He was just an alley cat, but he looked very friendly.

"Hi, there!" called the cat. "The name's Abraham Delacy Giuseppe Casey Thomas O'Malley. What's yours?"

"Duchess," she answered.

"Beautiful. Just like those blue eyes," O'Malley purred.

Duchess blushed. "Would you tell us how to get back to the city?"

"Tell you, fair lady?" replied O'Malley. "Why, I'll take you there on my magic carpet."

"Hooray!" cheered the kittens.

"One magic carpet, coming up!"
O'Malley shouted. He pointed to a milk
truck rattling down the road.

O'Malley jumped onto the front of the milk truck.

He hissed! He howled!

The truck screeched to a halt. The driver got out

of the truck to look for O'Malley.

"Where is that silly cat?" the driver wondered. He didn't see who was climbing into the back of his truck.

O'Malley's magic carpet had plenty of milk.
Duchess and the kittens enjoyed their breakfast. But
soon the driver noticed his passengers.

"Jump!" cried O'Malley. The cats jumped out of the milk truck.

"Don't worry," he told Duchess. "I'll make sure you get back home."

"Just follow me," said O'Malley. He led them through the pretty countryside.

"O'Malley is so smart," said Marie.

"O'Malley is so brave," said Toulouse.

"When I grow up," said Berlioz, "I am going to
be just like O'Malley."

They came to some railroad tracks. O'Malley
decided to follow the tracks to the city.

As they walked across a railroad bridge, the kittens pretended to be a train.

"*Choo-choo. Choo-choo,*" hummed Marie.

"*Clickety-clack. Clickety-clack,*" buzzed Berlioz.

"*Whoo-whoo!*" whistled Toulouse.

WHOO-WHOO! answered a real train—and it was right behind them!

"Don't panic!" shouted O'Malley.

Everyone got under the tracks just in time.

"Hold on, children!" Duchess called. But the
train shook the bridge, and Marie lost her grip.

"Mama!" she cried as she fell into
the cold water below.

O'Malley did a
daring dive . . .

. . . and quickly pulled Marie out
of the river.

"Thank you, Thomas," said
Duchess gratefully. "You have
saved my daughter's life."

Back in Paris, the newspapers confirmed that the cats had been catnapped! Roquefort was looking for clues. He was talking to Frou-Frou the horse when Edgar appeared. The butler seemed upset.

"My hat!" he cried. "If they find it, they'll know I'm the catnapper!"

Now Roquefort knew the truth. But where were his friends?

His friends were in Paris!

"We can stay in my penthouse pad for the night,"
O'Malley said. He led them up to the rooftops.

"Wow! This is great!" exclaimed Toulouse.

Music drifted out of an
open skylight.

"Listen to that music,"
said Berlioz.

"That's jazz," O'Malley told
him. "And those musicians are
friends of mine."

They went inside. O'Malley
introduced Duchess to Scat Cat
and the band.

O'Malley and Scat Cat
sang a song. Everyone
danced.

"It isn't
Beethoven, Mama,
but it sure bounces,"
giggled Berlioz.

"Let's swing it,
Thomas," laughed
Duchess. They had
lots of fun!

After the party was over, Duchess and O'Malley admired the full moon.

"I'm going to miss you, Beautiful. And those kittens, too," admitted O'Malley.

"We will miss you," Duchess said softly. "But tomorrow we must go home to Madame. I'm sure she's very worried."

"I guess you know best," sighed O'Malley.

The kittens were watching
from a window.

"Well, we almost had a father,"
Berlioz said quietly.

When Edgar opened the door the next morning,
he got the shock of his life. The cats had returned!

"Me first! Me first!" cried Marie. The kittens
ran into the house.

"I'll never forget you, Thomas O'Malley,"
purred Duchess.

"So long," the alley cat replied sadly.

As soon as the door was closed, Edgar put the cats in a sack!

"I'll send these cats to Timbuktu," he declared. Edgar locked them in a trunk in the barn. Then he left to call for a shipping van.

Luckily Roquefort had seen everything! The
brave mouse ran for help. He found O'Malley first.
O'Malley told the mouse to get Scat Cat and his band
to help, too.

When Edgar returned to the barn, he had a big
surprise waiting for him!

Scat Cat and his band took care of Edgar.
Meanwhile, Roquefort and O'Malley freed
Duchess and the kittens.

Duchess and the kittens quickly jumped out of the trunk. Then Frou-Frou pushed Edgar in!

After thanking their friends, Duchess and the kittens had a happy reunion with Madame. O'Malley went along. Since Duchess seemed fond of O'Malley, Madame invited him to stay.

The shipping van came. Edgar was driven off to Timbuktu!

Madame never saw him again. So she told her lawyer to change her will.

"Very well," said George. "Scratch one butler." And with a few more strokes of the pen, O'Malley was added to the will!

O'Malley was a very good father. With a bit of grooming, he was also a fine Aristocat. The cats made such a fine family that Madame decided to take a family picture.

"You know," Madame said. "If Edgar had only known about the will, I'm sure he never would have left. Especially since I've decided to open my home to all the cats of Paris."

Duchess and O'Malley just smiled.